Daddy Pig's Office

Today, as a special treat, Peppa and George are visiting Daddy Pig's office. "Daddy? Grunt. What do you do at your office all day?" asks Peppa.

"Lots of fun things!" replies Daddy Pig. "We're here!" he tells the children as they arrive at a very tall building.

"Hello!" says Daddy Pig into the intercom.
"Hello, Daddy Pig!" says a voice.
"Can I press the button?" Peppa asks.
"Ho, ho! Of course, Peppa!" Daddy replies.

Beep!

"My office is at the top.
We have to go up in the lift,"
Daddy Pig tells the children.
"Can I press the button? Snort!"
asks Peppa, excitedly.
"I think it's George's turn. Press the
top button please, George,"
says Daddy Pig.

The lift takes them to the top floor
"Hello, everyone!" grunts Daddy Pig.
"Hello," say Mr Rabbit and Mrs Cat.
They work with Daddy Pig.

"I have two special visitors with me today - Peppa and George!" says Daddy Pig.

"Let's begin a tour!" suggests Daddy Pig.
"Mr Rabbit, can we start at your desk?"
"We certainly can!" replies Mr Rabbit.
"My job is all about numbers."

Grunt!

Hee, hee, hee!

IN

"I take important pieces of paper and stamp them with a rubber stamp," Mr Rabbit tells them. "Wow!" gasp the children. Peppa likes stamping paper.

"Ho, ho! On with the tour! Next is Mrs Cat's desk!" exclaims Daddy Pig.

"Hello, Peppa and George," says Mrs Cat. "My job is all about drawing shapes on a computer."

"Can I try?" asks Peppa.
"I think it's George's turn,"
says Daddy Pig.
"Yes. It's your turn to work,
George," says Peppa.
"Snort," agrees George.
Mrs Cat helps George make
lots of blue triangles.

"Now we print the triangles out," Peppa cries.

The printer spits out sheets of paper everywhere!

"Hee, hee!" George and Peppa think it's hilarious.

"Do you want to see my desk?" Daddy Pig asks.

"Yes, please! Grunt!" says Peppa.

Clatter!
Clatter!
Clatter!

Daddy Pig's job is
very important.
"Do you use stamps or a
computer?" asks Peppa.
"No," replies Daddy Pig.
"I use coloured pens!"
Peppa and George love
colouring pens.

"George is drawing a dinosaur. George always draws dinosaurs," says Peppa, bored. "Dine-saw! Grrr!" says George.

"Ding, ding!" The office clock has just chimed.
"My goodness! Five o'clock already!" says Daddy Pig.
It is time for Peppa, George and Daddy to go home.

"You've been doing my job very well!" snorts Daddy Pig. "I like doing Mr Rabbit's job and I like doing Mrs Cat's job, but I like doing your job the best, Daddy," says Peppa. Peppa and George have had an excellent day at Daddy Pig's office.

$$x = \frac{-b \pm}{2}$$

**PARK
LEARNING CENTRE**

The Park, Cheltenham
Gloucestershire GL50 2QF
Telephone: 01242 532721

**UNIVERSITY OF
GLOUCESTERSHIRE**

WEEK LOAN

WEEK LOAN

-5 JUN 1998	12 JAN 2000	18 JAN 2002
23 JUN 1998	18 JAN 2000	13 MAY 2002
-6 NOV 1998	ILL On/P21	17 JAN 2003
ILL due 4/1/99	Due 10/2/2000	28 APR 2003
19 JAN 1999	25 OCT 2000	23 APR 2004
ILL due 12/3/99	-2 NOV 2000	29 APR 2004
ILL due 27/9/99	13 DEC 2000	
	13 FEB 2001	OCT 2004
SF/P-1	19 FEB 2001	14 JAN 2005
26 OCT 1999	26 FEB 2001	
-2 NOV 1999	-5 MAR 2001	
14 DEC 1999		

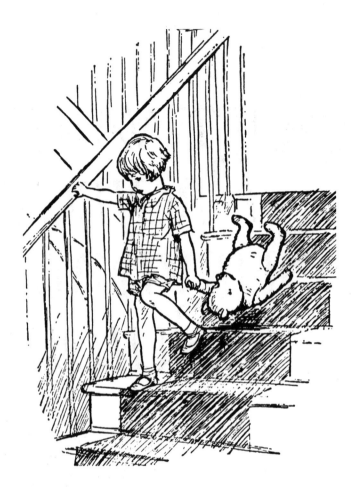

Here is Edward Bear, coming downstairs now, bump, bump, bump on the
back of his head, behind Christopher Robin.
It is, as far as he knows, the only way of coming downstairs,
but sometimes he feels that there really is another way,
if only he could stop bumping for a moment and think of it.
And then he feels that perhaps there isn't.